THE
APPLE-PIP
PRINCESS

For the children of Coldfall Primary School

First U.S. edition 2008

First published in Great Britain in 2007 by Orchard Books, London

Library of Congress Cataloging-in-Publication Data is available.

Library of Congress Catalog Card Number 2007034239

ISBN 978-0-7636-3747-7

10 11 12 13 14 SCP 10 9 8 7 6 5 4

Printed in Humen, Dongguan, China

This book was typeset in Stempel Schneidler.

Candlewick Press
99 Dover Street
Somerville, Massachusetts 02144

visit us at www.candlewick.com

THE APPLE-PIP PRINCESS

Jane Ray

CANDLEWICK PRESS

L et me tell you a story about something that happened a long time ago in a land far from here—a land ruled by an old king who had three daughters.

Their kingdom had once been covered in forests filled with birdsong, and the palace had been a busy and bustling place. But since the queen's death, the heart had gone out of the kingdom—the winters were bitter, the summers were scorched, and the palace was filled only with sadness.

The people lived in tumbledown cottages and scratched a living from the dry earth. The animals were so skinny you could hear their ribs rattling, and the birds were too hungry to sing.

Now, before the queen had died, she'd asked each of her daughters to choose one of her possessions to remember her by.

Suzanna, the eldest princess, picked a pair of fine scarlet shoes, with heels that made sparks on the cobblestones. When Suzanna put them on, she felt tall and important.

Miranda, the middle princess, chose a magnificent mirror made of silver and pearls. She spent hours gazing into it, thinking herself quite the most beautiful princess there had ever been.

Serenity, the youngest princess, chose only
a simple wooden box that she had
loved since she was a baby.

Inside the box were seven magical things
that the queen had collected when she was
a little girl.

There was a scattering of raindrops, a
splash of sunlight, a fragment of rainbow,
a starbird's feather, a spider's dewy web,
a burst of nightingale song, and, at the
bottom, an embroidered silken bag that
held a tiny apple pip.

Serenity liked to look
carefully at all the things inside.
They helped her remember her mother
and how beautiful their land had once been.

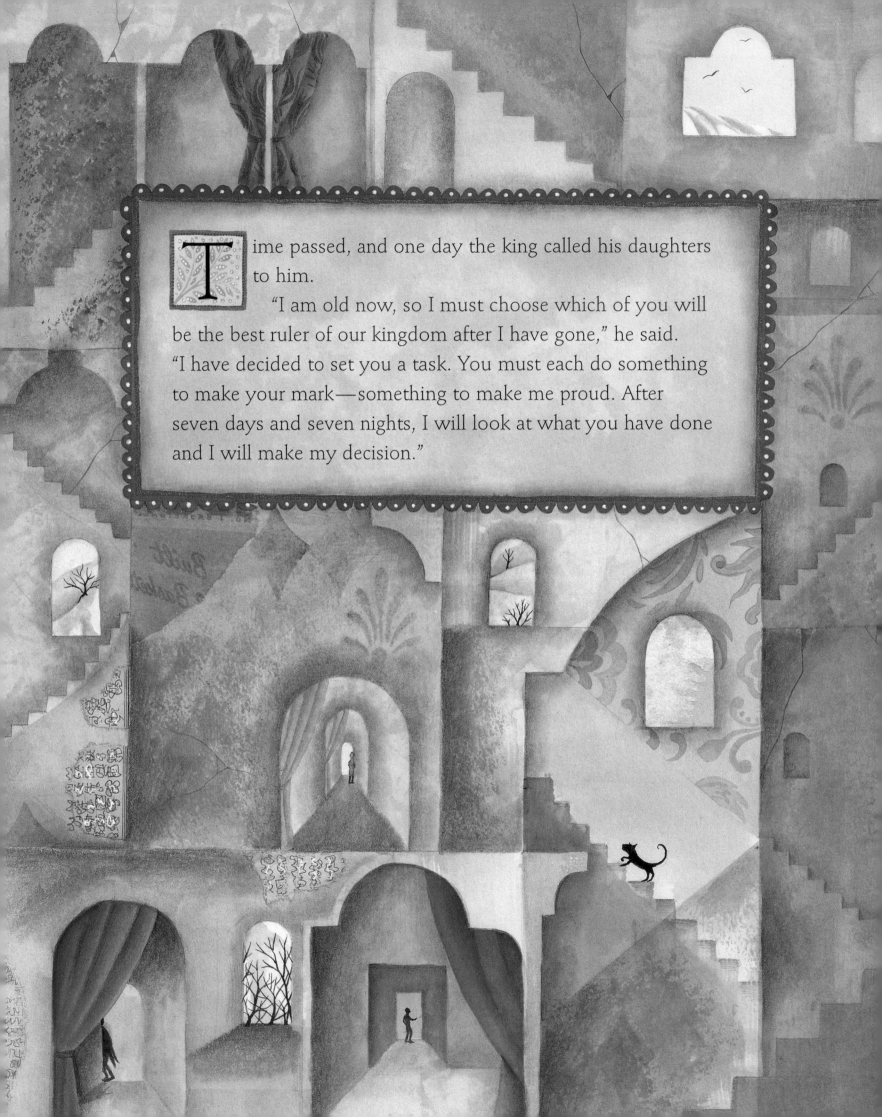

ime passed, and one day the king called his daughters to him.

"I am old now, so I must choose which of you will be the best ruler of our kingdom after I have gone," he said. "I have decided to set you a task. You must each do something to make your mark—something to make me proud. After seven days and seven nights, I will look at what you have done and I will make my decision."

Suzanna was clever and knew straightaway what she wanted to do. "I will build the tallest tower in the world," she said. "It will be so tall that it will reach the moon. People will see it and remember what a very important person I am. They will be so proud to be ruled by me that they won't mind being hungry at all."

She sent orders for people to bring her all the wood in the kingdom—even if it was the roof over their heads or the fences that kept their animals safe. And if anyone even thought of arguing with her, she would throw them into the dark and crumbling royal dungeon!

Miranda was clever, too, but rather vain and far too busy admiring herself in the mirror to have any ideas of her own.

"If Suzanna is building a tower tall enough to reach the moon, I will build one to reach the stars," said Miranda. "If her tower is made from plain old wood, mine will be made of shiny metal. People will see my lovely tower and remember how beautiful I am. They will be so honored to be ruled by me that they won't mind being poor at all!"

Immediately, Miranda sent orders for people to bring her all the metal in the kingdom—even their cooking pots and tin pans, copper bells and birdcages. And if anyone argued, Miranda would stamp her foot and throw them into the dark and crumbling royal dungeon!

Now, I expect you are wondering about Serenity, the youngest princess. Maybe you think that I'm going to tell you that she was the cleverest, or the most beautiful, or her father's favorite, because that is often the way with fairy tales.

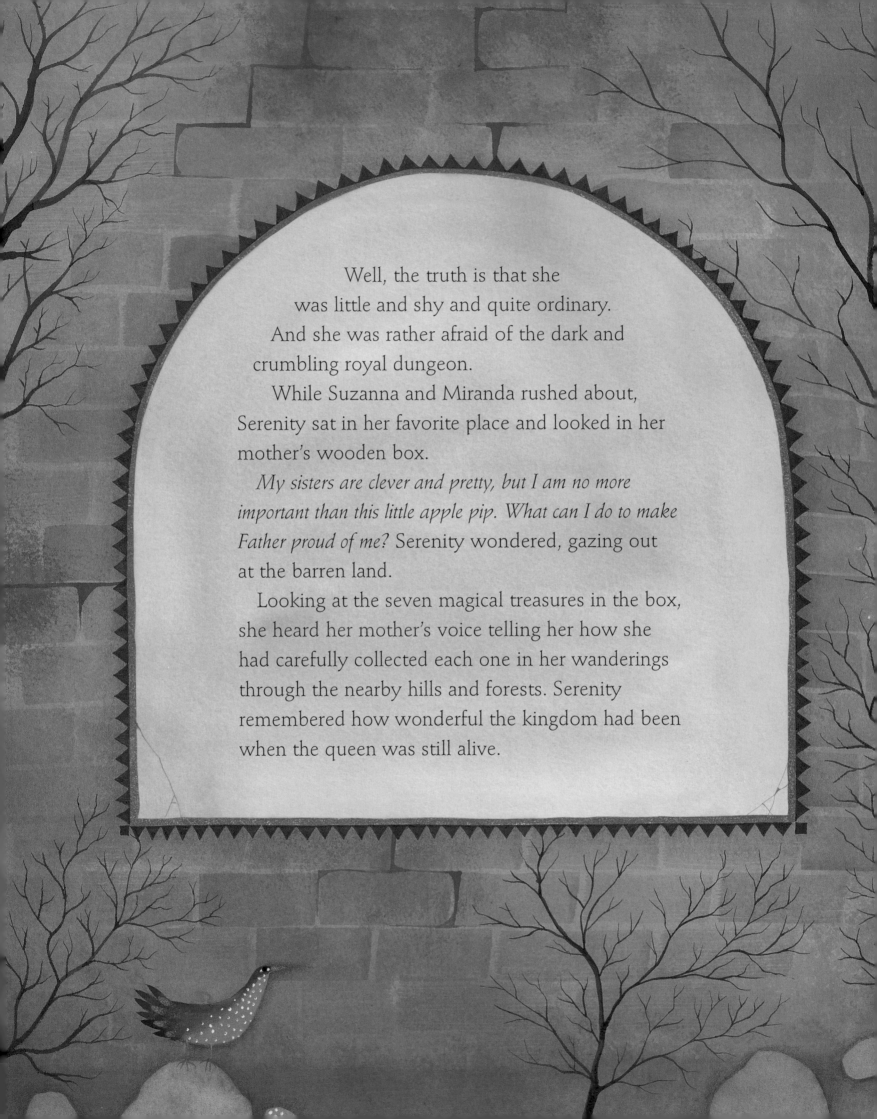

Well, the truth is that she
was little and shy and quite ordinary.
And she was rather afraid of the dark and
crumbling royal dungeon.

While Suzanna and Miranda rushed about,
Serenity sat in her favorite place and looked in her
mother's wooden box.

*My sisters are clever and pretty, but I am no more
important than this little apple pip. What can I do to make
Father proud of me?* Serenity wondered, gazing out
at the barren land.

Looking at the seven magical treasures in the box,
she heard her mother's voice telling her how she
had carefully collected each one in her wanderings
through the nearby hills and forests. Serenity
remembered how wonderful the kingdom had been
when the queen was still alive.

And slowly, the tiny seed of an amazing idea began
to form in her mind. She began to smile.
And then she began to work.

On the first day, Serenity took a trowel and began to dig in the
ground. It was difficult work, because the earth was baked
hard by the sun, but she kept digging until it was crumbly
and brown. Carefully, she took the tiny apple pip from its
embroidered bag and planted it in the earth.

On the second day, Serenity planted the pips from her breakfast pear next to the apple pip. Then, she watered them with the scattering of raindrops.

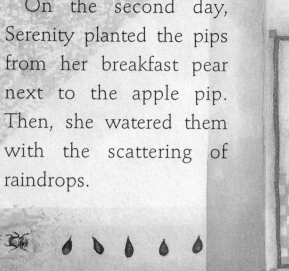

On the third day, she planted the pips from an orange she had for lunch and let the splash of sunlight dance over the earth. Then, she watched in amazement as green shoots pushed their way through the soil.

On the fourth day, Serenity planted pits from her suppertime cherries. Then, she took the fragment of rainbow and flung it high into the blue sky. The little green plants turned their leaves to the sun and smiled.

On the fifth day, Serenity noticed a boy from the village watching her and called him over. He brought her a plum pit and began to help. They worked together all day, digging in the hot sun, and by evening they were firm friends.

Before they went home, Serenity took the starbird's feather and let it fan a soft fresh breeze over the earth.

The boy's name was Joseph, and on the sixth day he returned
with olive pits from his mother. Word began to spread, and the
people came to offer gifts of orange and lemon pips.

They helped Serenity and Joseph dig and water, plant and sow,
and taught them all they remembered about tending the land.

Before the sun began to set, Serenity draped the spider's dewy
web over the bright young leaves and buds of the tiny apple tree.

By the seventh day, the land beyond the palace walls was covered in the misty green of little seedlings. But Serenity had a problem. Although she could easily imagine how lovely all the trees and plants would be when they were fully grown, she realized that they would never be ready when the king made his decision the next day.

As evening approached, Serenity suddenly put down her trowel. "It's no good," she said. "My father can't possibly choose me." "The plants will grow," Joseph said. "Look how strong the little apple tree has grown. We must just be patient."

Darkness fell, and Serenity was tired and despondent. With tears in her eyes, she opened the wooden box one last time and released the burst of nightingale song among the branches of the tiny apple tree.

With the beautiful sound filling their ears,
Serenity and Joseph fell into an exhausted sleep.

Early the next morning, the king appeared—it was time to make his decision.

Suzanna called to him from the top of her tower.

"Father, Father—look at this tower! Surely it's the tallest tower you've ever seen. I should definitely be the one to rule the kingdom!"

But the king shivered in the shadow that the huge tower cast.

"Father, Father—look at me!" called Miranda from the top of her tower. "Isn't this the most beautiful tower you have ever seen? I should rule the kingdom!"

But the king was blinded by the shiny tower flashing in the sun.

The king looked around for his youngest daughter, but she was nowhere to be seen. He walked outside the palace walls and found Serenity and Joseph lying asleep on the ground. He woke them gently.

"Oh, Father, I'm so sorry . . ." Serenity began, but the king took her by the shoulders and turned her around.

As far as her eyes could see, there were plants and trees—fruit, olive, and nut trees, all fresh and green in the early morning sunshine. Serenity and her father walked slowly, arm in arm.

The air was full of the scent of flowers, and all around them children were playing. People were picking fruit and tending the trees, and the old people were resting in the dappled shade.

The old king felt his poor unhappy heart fill with warmth again
as all his sadness drifted away on the breeze.
   "Serenity, my Serenity," he said. "You shall rule the kingdom!
For you have transformed the land and made it blossom again."

But what of Suzanna and Miranda, you ask? Well, if Suzanna stood at the very top of her creaking tower, on tiptoe in her scarlet shoes, and reached as high as she could, she could nearly touch the moon.

And if Miranda balanced on the very top turret of her shiny tower, she could nearly touch the stars.

But after a while, each began to feel rather lonely. Then they heard the sound of laughter and birdsong floating up on the breeze.

So they climbed down and joined the king, Serenity,
Joseph, and everyone else sitting under the trees.

As day faded into night, the three princesses lay down in the
grass and listened to the magical sound of the nightingale's song.